May We Sleep Here Tonight?

Tan Koide

Illustrated by Yasuko Koide

A MARGARET K. McELDERRY BOOK / ATHENEUM 1983 New York

Library of Congress catalog card number 82-72247 ISBN 0-689-50261-3
Text copyright © 1981 by Tan Koide   Illustrations copyright © 1981 by Yasuko Koide
All rights reserved   Printed in Japan   First American Edition
Originally published by Fukuinkan Shoten, Publishers, Tokyo, Japan, 1981

Three little gophers were out on a hike,
but on their way home they got lost. The sun
had set and fog was beginning to roll in.

The little gophers looked all around,
and in the distance, they saw a house.

"Let's see if we can sleep there tonight."

When they reached the house, the gophers took turns knocking on the door.

Tap. Tap. Tap.

"May we come in, please?"

But no matter how loudly they knocked, there was no answer.

Slowly, they opened the door. Nobody was at home.

"Who's house is this, anyway?" said one gopher.

"I wonder if it's rude to stay here without asking?" said another.

But the three little gophers were very tired.

So they all got into bed.

After a while, they heard the sound of footsteps.

Somebody was coming!

Knock. Knock.

"May we come in, please?"

Slowly, the door opened.

Two bunny rabbits peeked in from outside.

"We lost our way in the fog," they said. "May we sleep here tonight?"

"Surely, surely—come right in. We lost our way, too, and we're here just for the night," said the gophers.

So the two bunny rabbits got into bed with the little gophers.

After a while, they heard the sound of footsteps
again. Somebody else was coming!

Knock. Knock.

"May we come in, please?"

Suddenly, the door flew open.

Three raccoons rushed in.

"We're lost, we're lost," they exclaimed, "and we just saw something strange out there! May we sleep here tonight?"

"Of course, come in. We're all lost, too."

So the three gophers, the two bunny rabbits and
the three raccoons all got into bed together.
    But after a little while they heard a loud noise.
Could it be footsteps again?

This time there was no knock. No one asked if they
could come in. But *creak, creak*—the door was opened.

Something huge and black walked in. It came close to the bed and sniffed about, making funny noises through its nose. Somebody shivered. Then everyone shivered. Somebody started to cry. And soon everyone else did too.

Then, to their horror—

the huge, black monster lifted up the
bedcover and said, "Well, well, what
a lot of guests I have tonight."

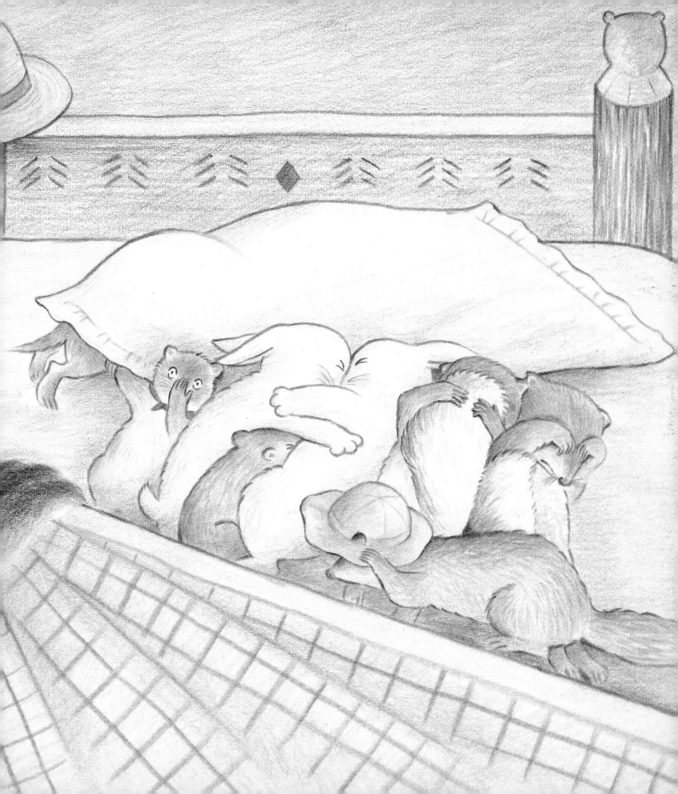

It was Mr. Bear, who lived in the house.

"I often put travelers up for the night when they've lost their way," he said, "and with the fog tonight, I went out searching, to see if anyone was in trouble. Now, warm up, lads, and make yourselves at home."

So saying, Mr. Bear ladled out some hot stew for everyone to eat.

And so, the three little gophers, two bunny rabbits, and three raccoons ate as much stew as their tummies would hold.

Then together with Mr. Bear, they got into bed and slept soundly till the morning.

1-3

E
Koide, Tan.
 May we sleep here tonight?

	DATE DUE	